Puffin Books

Time for a Story

Eileen Colwell was born in Yorkshire and began her career as a librarian in Bolton, Lancashire. She moved to London to found a library system for children in the Borough of Barnet, becoming its first librarian and eventually librarian-in-charge of all work with children and young people. She is known internationally for her story-telling and was one of the first story-tellers on *Playschool* and *Jackanory*, as well as a broadcaster in educational programmes. She had edited many collections of stories for children and written on children's literature and story-telling. In 1968 she was made an MBE and in 1976 was awarded the degree of Doctor of Letters by Loughborough University. In 1994 she won the Eleanor Farjeon Award for her services to children and children's literature

Today Eileen Colwell is still interested in the changing trends in children's literature and is actively involved in the resurgence of story-telling.

Compiled by Eileen Colwell
Illustrated by Charlotte Hough

Time for a Story

PUFFIN BOOKS

PUFFIN BOOKS

Published by the Penguin Group
Penguin Books Ltd, 27 Wrights Lane, London W8 5TZ, England
Penguin Books USA Inc., 375 Hudson Street, New York, New York 10014, USA
Penguin Books Australia Ltd, Ringwood, Victoria, Australia
Penguin Books Canada Ltd, 10 Alcorn Avenue, Toronto, Ontario, Canada M4V 3B2
Penguin Books (NZ) Ltd, 182–190 Wairau Road, Auckland 10, New Zealand

Penguin Books Ltd, Registered Offices: Harmondsworth, Middlesex, England

First published 1967
30 29 28 27 26 25 24 23

Set in Bembo Monotype
Typeset by Cox & Wyman Ltd, Reading
Printed in England by Clays Ltd, St Ives plc

Contents

Acknowledgements

Grateful acknowledgements are due to the following: Brockhampton Press Ltd and Leila Berg for 'The Dog That Had no Name' from *Lollipops*; Angus and Robertson Ltd and the Australian Broadcasting Company and Jean Chapman for 'Punchinello Kept a Cat' from *Listening Time*; Angus and Robertson and the Australian Broadcasting Company and Jill Meillon for 'The Traffic Jam' from *Listening Time*; Vera Colwell for 'The Puppet Show' and 'To the Stars'; Elizabeth Clark for 'The Tale of the Little Brown Bird' from *More Stories and How to Tell Them*; Mrs Beth Caples for several finger plays; Caroline D. Emerson for 'The Train That Wouldn't Stay on the Rails'; Glenys Evans for 'Chunky the China Pig'; Longmans Green and Company Ltd and J. Taylor and T. Ingleby for 'Bullawong' from *My Yellow Book*; Methuen and Company Ltd and Donald Bisset for 'The Quacking Pillarbox' and 'The Hot Potato' from *Some Time Stories*; J. Garnet Miller and Barbara Ker Wilson for 'Chocolate Kittens' and 'Huff and Puff' from *A Story to Tell*; Oliver and Boyd Ltd and Margaret Law for 'The First Snowdrop' and 'The Bus That Wouldn't Go' from *Stories to Tell to the Nursery* and 'The Little River' from *More Stories to Tell to the Nursery*; Sir Isaac Pitman and Sons Ltd and Kathleen Bartlett for 'The Apple Tree' and 'The Mouse in the Hole' from *Number Rhymes and Finger Plays*; Marjorie Poppleton for 'The Big Red Apple' from *Ten Tales for the Very Young*; Stephanie Sale for 'The Little Tiger who Didn't Like Washing'; Ursula Moray Williams for 'The Silver Horse'.

Huff and Puff

BY BARBARA KER WILSON

Two trains stood in the station. One was a smart Express Train, with lots of shiny green carriages stretched out behind its engine. The other was a shabby Goods Train, with a row of dusty trucks.

'Huff, huff, huff, huff!' the Express Train said proudly. 'I am going to the seaside. I am going to Sandy Bay. My carriages are filled with people travelling to their summer holidays.'

'Puff, puff, puff, puff!' the Goods Train said humbly. 'I am going to Sandy Bay too. My trucks are filled with useful things.'

'Old slowcoach!' said the Express Train scornfully. 'I shall be at the seaside long before you get there!'

This annoyed the Goods Train. 'Don't be too sure of that,' it said. 'I may get there first, for all you know.'

'*You* get there first?' exclaimed the Express Train. 'Huff!'

'Puff!' replied the Goods Train. 'Let's have a race and settle the argument that way.'

'Huff, huff!' cried the Express Train. 'A race with you? You haven't a hope of winning it!'

'Puff, puff,' said the Goods Train. 'Just wait and see!'

The Guard came along the station platform. He blew his whistle and waved his green flag.

'We're off!' said all the people in the Express Train. 'We'll soon be there! We'll soon be at Sandy Bay!'

'Here we go,' said the Goods Train's dusty trucks. 'We're going to the seaside too!'

And the two trains huffed and puffed out of the station.

The Express Train was soon out of sight. 'Soon be there, soon be there! Rattlety-tum, rattlety-tum!' sang all its shiny carriages.

The Goods Train chugged along slowly and steadily. 'Going-to-the-seaside, going-to-the-seaside,' chanted its dusty trucks.

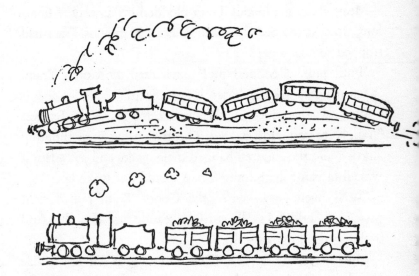

The sun shone in the blue sky. It was a very hot day. In the green fields beside the railway line, the sheep and cows were drowsy with the heat. By and by the Express Train began to feel sleepy too. 'Huff-a-huff!' it yawned. 'I do feel sleepy! I think I will take a little rest. That silly old Goods Train is a long way behind me. It will never catch me up now!' And it stopped suddenly.

'What's happened?' said all the people in the shiny carriages. 'Why has the train stopped? Express Trains should never stop until they reach their stations. Wake up, wake up! Take us to Sandy Bay!'

But the Express Train did not hear them. It was fast asleep.

13

Meanwhile, the Goods Train plodded on its way. After a long time, it reached the place where the Express Train had stopped to take a nap.

'Puff, puff! Goodness me!' exclaimed the Goods Train. 'That naughty Express Train is fast asleep!'

By now, the people in the shiny carriages of the Express Train were very cross indeed. The grown-ups were shouting angrily, and the children banged their spades and pails. But it was all in vain: the Express Train would not wake up.

'Well, well; well, well,' the Goods Train puffed as it passed by. 'I think I shall get to the seaside first after all!' And it chugged on out of sight.

Much later, the Express Train woke up. It did not realize how long it had been asleep. The sun was still shining in the sky, and the cows and sheep were still grazing in the green fields beside the railway line. Then it heard all the people complaining.

'What a fuss to make!' snorted the Express Train. 'People are so impatient! Why, I only closed my eyes for a few moments! As for that stupid old Goods Train, it must be miles behind me still!'

Then it started on its way again: rattlety-tum, rattlety-tum. '*Wheeeee!*' its whistle blew as it rattled through a tunnel. 'Look out everyone. Here I come!'

At last the Express Train reached Sandy Bay. 'We can see the sea! Look at the yellow sands!' cried all the people in the shiny carriages. The Express Train drew into the station, and stopped beside the platform.

'Here I am!' it huffed proudly.

'Oh, *there* you are at last!' said another voice. It was the Goods Train who had been waiting at the station for a long time.

The Express Train stared at the Goods Train in astonishment. 'It can't be you!' it cried. 'It's impossible! Oh huff!'

'Oh puff!' said the Goods Train. 'It *is* me. I got here first, you see!'

'Huff, huff,' the Express Train sniffed sadly, 'you must have passed me while I snoozed.'

'Puff, puff,' said the Goods Train kindly. 'You should keep going, like me. I'm slow but sure!'

From *A Story to Tell*

Bullawong

BY J. TAYLOR AND T. INGLEBY

Bullawong is a river, a very wide brown river in a very hot country.

One day a little boy was walking by the river and he sang this song as he walked along:

> 'I will sing you a song,
> Bullawong, Bullawong.
> As you flow along
> I will sing you a song.'

Bullawong then spoke, and he said, 'Are you hot, Boy?'

'Yes, I am very hot,' said the little boy.

'Then dive into my waters,' said Bullawong. So the little boy dived into the waters of the river Bullawong.

'Do you like my waters?' asked the river.

'Yes,' said the little boy, 'your waters are swift and cool.' And he swam about and he sang:

> 'I will sing you a song,
> Bullawong, Bullawong.
> As you flow along
> I will sing you a song.'

Bullawong then spoke, and he said, 'Are you hungry, Boy?'

'Yes, I am very hungry,' said the little boy.

'Then I will send you fish. Look in front of you and you will see a pool with many silver fish.'

So the little boy looked in front, and in the pool he caught a silver fish and he ate it.

'Do you like my silver fish?' asked the river.

'Yes,' said the little boy, 'it was very good.' And he swam about and he sang:

'I will sing you a song,
    Bullawong, Bullawong.

As you flow along
I will sing you a song.'

Bullawong then spoke, and he said, 'Are you thirsty, Boy?'

'Yes, I am very thirsty,' said the little boy.

'Then I will send you water to drink. Look to the right bank, and you will see a crystal stream that flows into my waters.'

So the little boy looked to the right, and he drank of the crystal stream.

'Do you like my crystal stream?' asked the river.

'Yes,' said the little boy, 'it is clear and fresh.' And he swam about and he sang:

'I will sing you a song,
Bullawong, Bullawong.
As you flow along
I will sing you a song.'

Bullawong then spoke, and he said, 'Are you strong, Boy?'

'Yes, I am very strong,' said the little boy.

'Then I will send you waves to fight. Look behind you and you will see wild waves rushing at you.'

So the little boy looked behind, and he dived into the waves and broke them.

'Do you like my waves?' asked the river.

'Yes,' said the little boy, 'they are wild and rolling.' And he swam about and he sang:

'I will sing you a song,
  Bullawong, Bullawong.
  As you flow along
  I will sing you a song.'

Bullawong then spoke, and he said, 'Are you tired, Boy?'

'Yes, I am very tired,' said the little boy.

'Then I will find you a cradle. Look to the left bank and you will see a boat tied up by a tree.'

So the little boy looked to the left bank and he climbed into the boat and lay down to rest.

'Do you like my boat?' asked the river.

'Yes,' said the little boy, 'it is very pleasant.' And he closed his eyes and he sang:

19

'I will sing you a song,
Bullawong, Bullawong.
As you flow along . . . '

'Are you asleep, Boy?' asked the river. But the little boy did not answer. He was fast asleep.

So Bullawong rocked the boat to and fro, to and fro.

From *My Yellow Book*

1, 2, 3, 4, 5. Once I caught a fish alive.
6, 7, 8, 9, 10. But I let it go again.
Why did you let it go?
Because it bit my finger so.
Which finger did it bite?
This little finger on the right.

The Frog, the Cat and the Little Red Hen

TRADITIONAL

Once upon a time a Frog, a Cat and a little Red Hen lived together in a little house. The Frog and the Cat were lazy and selfish, so the little Red Hen, who was kind, did all the work each day.

One morning she said, 'Who will light the fire?'

'I won't,' said the Frog, yawning.

'I won't,' said the Cat, snuggling down into bed.

So the little Red Hen put on her apron, laid the fire and lighted it. Soon it was burning brightly and the room was warm.

'Who will sweep and dust while the oven is getting hot?' asked the little Red Hen.

'Not I,' said the Frog.

'Not I,' said the Cat.

So the little Red Hen swept and dusted the room and when it was all clean and tidy, she asked, 'Who will bake the bread for breakfast?'

'I shan't,' said the Frog, beginning to snore.

'I shan't,' said the Cat, tucking her tail under the eiderdown.

So the little Red Hen made a fine round loaf and put it in the oven to bake.

'Who will set the table while the bread is baking?' asked the little Red Hen.

'I won't,' said the Frog.

'I won't,' said the Cat.

So the little Red Hen set the table – a cup and saucer, a plate and a knife for each one and some creamy yellow butter.

Then she took the crusty loaf out of the oven.

'Who is hungry?' asked the little Red Hen.

'I am!' said the Frog, jumping out of bed.

'I am!' said the Cat, sitting down on her chair.

'So am I!' said the little Red Hen and, tucking the crusty loaf under her wing, she ran out of the door.

And I am glad to say she ate all that loaf herself.

The Train That Wouldn't Stay on the Rails

BY CAROLINE D. EMERSON

Once upon a time there was a train that was tired of staying on the rails.

'Why must I run on rails all the days of my life?' asked the train.

'You had much better stay where you are,' said the rails. 'We were laid for you to run on and you were made to run on us. Everything is better off in this world if it stays where it belongs.'

But the train would not listen.

'I'm not going to stay here,' he said and he jumped off the rails and began to run along the road.

'Keep off!' cried the cars. 'This road was made for us. Keep off! Keep off!'

'No such thing!' said the train. 'There's plenty of room on the road for me.'

He ran down the road. He stopped at the houses for people and their trunks and he stopped at the post office for the mail bags. He ran out to the farms for the milk. Everyone was delighted. It was much easier than to carry everything down to the station. But the train took so long that he never got to the end of his trip!

People waited for their trunks and they never came. The letters in the mail bags were so old that no one troubled to read them. The milk was sour and was no good to anyone. People stopped putting their things on to the train and began to send them by road instead.

'There now,' said the cars, 'no one is using you any more. You should have stayed on your rails as we told you to. The road is no place for you.'

But the train refused to go back to the rails. One day he saw a horse running across the fields.

'Why should I stay on a road?' asked the train. 'That looks like fun.'

He left the road and started off across the field.

'You mustn't come here,' cried the horse. 'This is my field. Keep off! Keep off!'

'No such thing,' answered the train, 'there's plenty of room in this field for me.'

Bump, bump, bump went the train across the field until he came to a stream.

'How do I get over this?' asked the train.

'Jump,' said the horse.

'I never jumped in my life,' said the train. 'I always have bridges built for me.'

'Bridges?' laughed the horse. 'You'd better go back where you belong. The rails are the place for you.'

But the train paid no attention to him for just then he heard an aeroplane up in the air.

'That looks like fun,' said the train. '*Why* should I stay on the ground? I'm going to fly.'

'Silly,' said the horse, 'you, who can't even jump a stream.'

The train tried to fly. He tried with his front wheels. He tried with his back wheels. He tried with all his wheels. He tried until he was tired.

'Well,' said the train, 'there appears to be something wrong. I can't fly. People won't ride on me when I bump across the fields and they won't send trunks and post by me when I run on the road. They say I'm too slow. I don't seem to be good for anything. I might as well stay right here. No one would miss me!'

The train felt lonely and discouraged. He felt he was no longer of any use in the world. Then an idea flashed through his valves.

'I might go back to my rails,' he thought. 'I wonder if they're still there?'

He crept across the field and down the road to the station. There lay the rails where he had left them, stretching off in both directions. They looked so safe and smooth! The train gave a great puff of happiness as he climbed back on to them.

'It's been lonely without you,' said the rails. 'We were afraid we'd rust away with no one running over us.'

At the station there were many people waiting and a pile of trunks and mail bags.

'This is just where I belong,' whistled the train cheerfully. And from that time on the little train could be seen every day running happily down the rails as smoothly as could be.

From *Read Me Another Story*

The First Snowdrop

BY MARGARET LAW

One day a little white flower pushed up out of the brown earth. She was a very small white flower and when she looked round about her she could see nothing but the dark earth from which she had come. There were no other flowers to keep her company. She was all alone.

'Perhaps I should have stayed where I was,' she said. 'All my sisters have waited below where they are safe and warm,' and she trembled as the cold wind blew over her.

Just then she heard a little brown bird singing in the tree above her head.

'Trill, trill,' sang the little brown bird. 'Look! Look! There's the first snowdrop. Spring is coming! Spring is coming! Trill, trill, trill.'

'Why,' said the flower, 'I believe the little brown bird is singing about me. I'm glad he seems so pleased to see me,' and she shook out her petals.

As she did so she saw a boy and girl running over the grass. They stopped when they came to the place where the flower was growing. 'Look! Look!' they cried. 'It's the first snow-drop – the very first one,' and they bent down and put their faces close to the little flower.

'How glad we are you have come,' they said. 'Now we know Spring is on the way. We must run and tell Mother we have seen you.' And off they went.

'Why,' said the flower, 'they seem pleased to see me too. I don't feel the cold any longer,' and she swung merrily on her green stalk.

Almost before the children were out of sight, an old gardener came slowly along, sweeping the paths clear of mud and paper. He stopped when he saw the little white flower, and leaned on his brush to look at her.

'Ah, here you are at last,' he said. 'Come to tell me Spring will soon be here, have you?' He knelt down and moved the old brown leaves out of the way. 'There now, we'll soon have your sisters up beside you,' and he smiled at the little white flower before he moved on.

Then out came the sun from behind a cloud where he had been hiding. 'Why, I believe that's a snowdrop down there,' he said. 'I shall send my sunbeams to give her a welcome.' So he shone down warmly on the dark brown earth till everything looked bright and gay.

'How right I was to push up out of the earth without waiting for my sisters,' said the little white flower. 'Everyone is so glad to see me. I have made people happy with my good news. Spring is coming! Spring is coming!' and she danced merrily in the sunshine.

From *Stories to Tell to the Nursery*

The Pigeon's Song

Coo-pe-coo. Coo-pe-coo,
Me and my poor two;
Two sticks across,
And a little bit of moss,
And it will do, do, do.

ANON.

Easter Chickens

BY EILEEN COLWELL

Janet was looking in the window of the sweet-shop. It was full of Easter eggs.

'Which would you like, darling?' asked her mother.

Janet had made up her mind already. Right in the middle of the window was a chocolate egg with a blue ribbon round it

and out of the egg was peeping a tiny yellow chick. This was the one she wanted!

So the egg was bought and Janet carried it home very carefully, in case the chick should be shaken out of the egg.

She went into the garden to look for her father. 'Look, Daddy,' she said, 'isn't it a dear little chicken!'

'It is indeed!' said her father, putting down the hammer he had in his hand so as to look better.

33

'What are you making, Daddy?' asked Janet. 'Is it a little house?'

'Ah, that's a secret!' said her father. 'But come along, I've been waiting for you. We're going for a drive in the country.'

'Where to?' asked Janet.

'That's a secret too!' her father teased.

Out in the country it was Spring. The trees were turning green, the birds were singing and the white lambs in the fields were growing quite big.

The car turned into a farm gate. The farmer seemed to be expecting them and he took them into the orchard. In a far corner under an apple tree covered with pink blossom, was a little wooden house with a wired-off run in front of it. Inside the house was a fat brown hen with several chickens.

'Oh, look!' exclaimed Janet. 'Easter chickens, just like mine!'

The chickens were little yellow fluffy balls. They ran about while their mother clucked anxiously, calling them to come under her wing.

'There you are,' said the farmer. 'Will they do?'

'Oh, Daddy,' said Janet, 'are we taking them home? Is that why you were building a little house?'

The farmer put the hen into a basket, but just as he was popping the chickens in with her, one of them ran away into the grass.

'Now where has the little creature gone?' said the farmer,

peering into the long grass. They could all hear the chicken *peeping* somewhere.

'I see it,' said Janet. 'It's in a hole at the bottom of the wall.'

The farmer stooped to look. 'I can't get my big hand in there,' he said. 'The silly little thing is too frightened to come out. Do you think you can reach it, my dear?'

Janet knelt down in the grass and put her hand into the hole very gently. 'Come along, chick,' she said softly. 'I won't hurt you.' Her hand closed over it and she lifted it out. It was soft and very tiny and it snuggled down into her hand and said *peep* in a sleepy kind of way.

'It likes me!' said Janet proudly and she put it into the basket with its mother.

So that Easter, Janet had two Easter chickens, a make-believe one and a real one.

The Quacking Pillarbox

BY DONALD BISSET

Once upon a time there was a pillarbox. He was very beautiful and held the letters safely inside him until the postman came to collect them.

Very close to the pillarbox there stood a lamp. They were great friends.

The lamp shone in the dark so that people could see their way home, and could see to post their letters.

One night the lamp said to the pillarbox: 'I believe I've caught a cold, I'm going to sneeze.'

And he sneezed so hard his light went out.

Now nobody could see to post their letters. What were they to do?

Just then a duck was walking by.

Her name was Miranda. She thought, 'Dear me! the lamp has gone out, how will people know where the pillarbox is, so as to post their letters?'

She climbed on top of the pillarbox and started quacking. She quacked and quacked and quacked, and all the people who were coming to post their letters, and couldn't find the pillarbox because the lamp was out, thought: 'Whatever is all that quacking for?'

They went to see where the noise was and saw Miranda quacking, and there, underneath Miranda, was the pillarbox. So they posted their letters in it and went home.

From *Some Time Stories*

Fun with your Fingers

Here is a tree with leaves so green,
  (Stretch arms sideways)
Here are the apples that hang between,
  (Clench fists)
When the wind blows, the apples will fall,
  (Clap hands)
Here is a basket to gather them all.
  (Fingers interlocking)

A little Mouse hid in a hole,
Hid softly in a little hole,
   (One finger – the mouse – hides in the other hand – the hole)
When all was quiet as quiet can be,
OUT
    POPPED
      HE!
   (The last three words are shouted and out pops the mouse)

Build the house up very high,
  (Fists on top of each other)
Point the chimney to the sky,
  (Point index fingers upwards)
Put the roof on,
  (Fingers meet at tips)
Lay the floor,
  (Fingers meet horizontally)
Open wide the big front door.
  (Fling arms wide in welcoming gesture)

Ten little soldiers standing in a row,
  (Show ten fingers)
They all bow down to their Captain so,
  (Close and open fingers)
They march to the left,
They march to the right,
They march straight home
  (Suit actions to the words)
And sleep all night.
  (Shut eyes, hands together under cheek)

There's a big-eyed owl
  (Forefingers and thumbs form circle round eyes)
With a pointed nose,
  (Fingers make V over nose)
Two pointed ears
  (Forefingers in front of ears)
And claws for his toes.
  (Fingers bent like claws)
He sits in a tree
And looks at you,
And flaps his wings
  (Wave arms)
And cries Whoo-hoo.
  (Hoot)

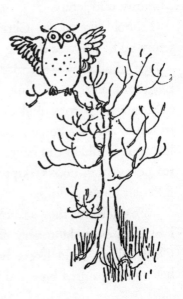

Chocolate Kittens

BY BARBARA KER WILSON

Christopher was Jenny's little brother. Jenny was four years old. Christopher was nearly three. Next Wednesday was his birthday.

On Tuesday, Mummy and Jenny went shopping together. Christopher stayed at home with Granny.

'I am going to buy a birthday present for Christopher,' Mummy told Jenny.

'I should like to buy Christopher a birthday present too,' Jenny said. 'I have a shilling in my purse.'

First of all they went to the toy-shop. The toy-shop was filled with all sorts of things a little boy would like to have: helicopters, tractors, pull-along trucks, motor-cars, lorries, tricycles, and big bouncy balls. There were lots of things a little girl would like to have, too: dolls' prams, spinning tops, magic painting-books, skipping-ropes and a whole shelf of different kinds of dolls.

'What a lot of things to choose from,' Mummy said. She looked at everything very carefully, and at last she decided Christopher would like a helicopter best. She chose a big helicopter, painted blue and white, with four blades. When you wound it up with a key, the blades whizzed round and round, and the helicopter moved along the floor.

'I will buy this helicopter,' Mummy told the toy-shop man. He put the helicopter in a box.

Then Mummy asked Jenny if she had decided what birthday present she would like to buy for Christopher.

'Yes, I have,' said Jenny. 'I would like to buy him a box of chocolate animals.'

'Then we must go to the sweet-shop,' said Mummy.

The sweet-shop was filled with good things to eat: chocolate to munch, toffee to chew, and lollipops and peppermints and fruit drops to suck.

Jenny went up to the counter.

'What would you like to buy, little girl?' asked the sweet-shop woman.

'A box of chocolate animals,' said Jenny. 'It is a birthday present for my brother.'

'What sort of chocolate animals would he like best?' asked the sweet-shop woman. 'There are chocolate kittens, chocolate rabbits, chocolate elephants and chocolate fishes.'

'I think Christopher would like chocolate kittens best,' said Jenny. 'How much money does a box of chocolate kittens cost?'

'One shilling,' said the sweet-shop woman.

So Jenny took the shilling out of her purse and the sweet-shop woman gave her a box of chocolate kittens.

'There are eight chocolate kittens in the box,' she told Jenny.

When they got home, Mummy hid the helicopter in a cupboard, and Jenny hid the box of chocolate kittens in her drawer in her bedroom. On the outside of the box there was a picture of a kitten playing with a ball of wool. 'That looks just like Tibbles when she was a little kitten,' thought Jenny. Tibbles was the family cat. Now she had grown into a plump black cat with long white whiskers.

When Jenny went to bed that night, she did not shut her eyes and go straight to sleep. What was the matter with Jenny? Why could she not go to sleep? She could see that box of chocolate kittens.

'How I should like to eat one little chocolate kitten,' thought Jenny. 'There are eight kittens in the box. I am sure Christopher would not mind if I ate just one!'

She got out of bed and tiptoed over to the dressing-table. She opened the box, took out one chocolate kitten, and popped it into her mouth. Mmn! How good it tasted! Then she got back into bed.

But still Jenny could not go to sleep. What was the matter now? She kept thinking about the seven chocolate kittens left inside the box. 'I am sure Christopher would not mind if I take just one more kitten,' she thought. 'The first kitten must be feeling lonely all by itself in my tummy!'

So she got out of bed a second time, opened the box, and

popped *another* chocolate kitten into her mouth. Mmn! Mmn! How good it tasted! Then Jenny went to bed once more.

But still she did not shut her eyes. She could not forget the six kittens left inside the box. I expect you can guess what happened next! Jenny got out of bed again, and ate a *third* chocolate kitten. Mmn! Mmn! Mmn! How good it tasted!

I am sorry to say that before long, there were NO CHOCOLATE KITTENS left inside the box at all.

47

Jenny had eaten every one! The box was empty. And at last, feeling rather sick, Jenny shut her eyes, and went to sleep.

The next day was Christopher's birthday. Daddy gave him a green tip-up lorry, Granny gave him a torch that shone with three different colours: green, yellow and red. Mummy gave him the blue and white helicopter. She wound it up with the key, and it ran all over the floor, its blades whizzing round and round.

'Jenny has a present for Christopher too,' Mummy said.

Jenny felt very ashamed of herself. She held out the box that had held the chocolate kittens. 'Here you are, Christopher,' she said in a small voice.

'Chocolate kittens! Mmn!' said Christopher. He opened the box. You can guess how disappointed he was when he found it was empty!

'My goodness!' said Mummy, 'where are all those chocolate kittens that were inside the box?'

'I think I know where they are,' said Granny. 'They are inside Jenny's tummy!'

'Oh, *Jenny!*' said Mummy.

'I'm sorry,' sobbed Jenny. 'Really I am!'

At that moment, Daddy came into the room. 'Come and see what Tibbles has for Christopher's birthday!' he said.

Everyone followed Daddy into the kitchen. There lay Tibbles in her basket. She was purring proudly. And beside her lay three fluffy black balls, Tibbles's very own kittens!

48

Christopher was very excited. 'Real life kittens are much better than chocolate ones!' he said.

'Cheer up, Jenny,' said Mummy. 'Clever Tibbles has made everything all right!'

From *A Story to Tell*

The Dog That Had no Name

BY LEILA BERG

Once upon a time there was a dog.

He was a very jolly dog, a yellow dog, and his nose was black. He had two white paws and two brown paws. But he had no name at all.

One day the little yellow dog said to himself: 'Everyone has a name but me. I shall go off and find a name.' So off he went.

He trotted down the street, and he passed some men mending the road. 'Hello, little yellow dog,' they shouted. 'Where are you off to, in such a hurry?'

'I'm off to find my name,' said the little yellow dog.

'Stop a minute,' cried the men. 'Is Pat your name?'

'No, Pat isn't my name,' said the little yellow dog. And he went on running.

He ran down the street, till he passed a lady buying bread. 'Hello, little yellow dog,' she said. 'Where are you running, so far away?'

'I'm off to find my name,' said the yellow dog.

'Wait a bit,' cried the lady. 'Is Bess your name?'

'No, Bess isn't my name,' said the little yellow dog. And he went on running.

He ran and ran, till he came to a window-cleaner carrying a ladder. 'Hello, little yellow dog,' cried the window-cleaner. 'Where are you off to, this fine day?'

'I'm off to find my name,' said the little yellow dog.

'Don't go so fast,' said the window-cleaner. 'Is Gyp your name?'

'No, Gyp isn't my name,' said the little yellow dog. And he went on running.

Then he ran and ran till he came to a postman carrying letters.

'Hello, little yellow dog,' said the postman. 'Where are you going at such a rate?'

'I'm going to find my name,' said the yellow dog.

'Is Rough your name?' asked the postman.

'No, Rough isn't my name,' said the little yellow dog. And he went on running.

He ran and ran, till he was tired out. Then he sat down on

the pavement and he stuck out his tongue. And he huffed, and huffed, and huffed, and huffed.

'Oh!' he said. 'I'll-never-find-my-name.'

Just then two little children came along. A boy and a girl.

'Hello, little yellow dog,' they said. 'You look quite tired out. Whatever have you been doing?'

'Huff!' said the little yellow dog. 'I've been looking for my name. But I haven't found it yet. And I'm very tired. Huff!'

'Wait a second,' said the children. 'I bet Trix is your name.'

The little dog thought for a moment. First he put his head on one side, and thought that way. Then he put his head on the other side, and thought that way. Then he stood up and wagged his tail. Then he turned round quickly three times.

'Yes,' he said. 'I bet it is. Trix is my name.'

'Hooray,' shouted the children. 'Then you can come with us.'

And off they ran, shouting and singing, the little girl, the little boy and the little yellow dog.

From *Lollipops*

The Puppet Show

BY VERA COLWELL

Just after Christmas, David's best friend John asked him to his party.

'John says that there is going to be a puppet show at his party,' said David to his mother. 'Will the puppets be like the ones on television?'

'Something like them, I expect,' said his mother, 'but these will be *real* ones, not just pictures. Puppets are fun!'

The party was just for boys and three more of David's friends were there. The rooms were still gay with Christmas decorations and the boys played exciting games and made a lot of noise. But David hadn't forgotten about the puppet show. 'Will it be soon?' he asked.

'Yes,' said John's mother, 'but tea first!'

'Hooray!' said the boys, for they were hungry after all the rushing about. It was a wonderful tea and David enjoyed it so much that even he forgot about the puppets for a time. But at last everyone had had enough and John led them into another room where some chairs were set out in front of what looked like a tall box. On the top of it was a tiny stage with the curtains drawn across.

The room went dark. Coloured lights appeared in front of

53

the stage and the curtains drew back. What could be going to happen, wondered David. This was much more exciting than puppets on television.

At the back of the stage was a house with two doors.

'Hello, boys!' said a voice and out of one of the doors popped a clown with a funny painted face, baggy trousers and coat and a pointed cap with red bobbles on it. 'I'm Bonzo the Clown,' he said. 'Shall I do some tricks?'

54

'Yes, please,' said the boys.

'Can't hear you!' said Bonzo.

'YES, PLEASE,' shouted the boys.

'That's better,' said Bonzo and began to do all kinds of funny things. He balanced a ball on his nose, he fell over in a comical way and he got tangled up in a string of sausages. Then he brought in a box and out of it jumped a Jack-in-a-Box. Bonzo pushed down the lid, and even sat on it, but the moment his back was turned, the Jack-in-a-Box bobbed up again in such a cheeky way that the boys were quite helpless with laughter.

'Sh-sh-sh!' said Bonzo. 'One of the circus tigers has got loose. I'm going to hide. Tell me if the tiger comes, won't you?' and he popped out of the door.

Then as the boys watched, the other door opened slowly and first a nose, then a whisker, then an ear appeared and a fierce-looking tiger came in. 'Gr-rr-rr!' it said. At that very moment, Bonzo opened the other door.

'The tiger!' shouted David and all the other boys. 'Look out, Bonzo!'

'Help!' said Bonzo and popped out quickly. In he came again, this time with a stick in his hand. Then began a most exciting time, for the tiger and Bonzo chased each other to and fro. The doors banged, Bonzo tried to hit the tiger – but he always missed – the tiger growled and the boys cheered. But at last Bonzo whacked the tiger on the head with his stick

55

and tied it up with the string of sausages. As he carried it off over his shoulder, David distinctly saw the tiger wave its paw. He was glad – he liked the tiger!

'Will there be some more?' he asked John.

'Lots!' said John. 'You wait and see!'

Three little pig-puppets came jigging in and acted the story of the 'Three Little Pigs' and the houses they built. The Wolf huffed and puffed down the chimney and the two houses fell, but the third little Pig's house stood up splendidly and the wicked Wolf fell down the chimney into the cooking-pot.

'Hooray!' shouted the boys.

Last of all, Bonzo came on the stage again. 'Time for you to go home,' he said.

'Oh!' said the boys sadly.

'Well, one more game with balloons, but that must be the last. There's a balloon for each of you, but someone must help me to give them out.'

'I will, I will,' shouted everyone, jumping up.

'I only need one boy,' said Bonzo. 'I'll choose the boy in the front row, the one with red hair.'

John poked David. 'He means you,' he whispered. 'Go on!'

'Me!' gasped David. 'Does he really mean me?'

'Of course, silly!' said John and gave him a push.

David went out to the front. He felt very proud. Fancy Bonzo choosing *him* to help!

One by one Bonzo dropped gay balloons over the edge of the stage. David caught most of them, but when he missed he laughed as much as the other boys. At last each boy had a balloon and began to play. All except David.

'Thank you for helping,' said a voice and Bonzo leaned over the edge of the stage and held out his hand to David! David reached up and took it – it was very small and felt like wood, but was it really made of wood? He watched the puppet go through the door at the back of the stage for the last time.

'Come on, David!' said one of the boys. 'Catch!' In a

moment David was running with the rest, knocking the balloons about and shouting with excitement. In the middle of the fun, David peeped into the room again half expecting to see Bonzo or the three little pigs watching.

There was no one there. The tall box had gone. The puppets had disappeared. In their place was a man he had never seen before.

'Was it a good show?' asked the man.

'Oh yes!' said David. 'But where has Bonzo gone?'

'I wonder,' said the man. 'Perhaps you'll meet him again some time.'

'I do hope I will,' said David, and he ran off home to tell his mother all about the wonderful Puppet Show.

The Little River

BY MARGARET LAW

Once upon a time a little river came tumbling down the hillside. Gurgle, gurgle, splash, splash, plop it sang as it ran along over the stones. Gurgle, gurgle, splash, splash, plop!

'Where are you going in such a hurry?' asked a blackbird who was hopping about on the branches of a tree. 'Stop for a little and speak to me. I want to know what grows at the top of the hill.'

'Nothing but grass! Nothing but grass!' shouted the river. 'That's all that grows at the top of the hill, and I can't tell you where I'm going, I'm sorry, because I don't know myself. I'm hurrying to find out. Good-bye.' And on he went – gurgle, gurgle, splash, splash, plop.

A sheep who was eating grass looked up as he passed. 'Where are you going in such a hurry?' he said. 'Have you come a long way? Stop a while and speak to me.'

'A very long way! A very long way!' shouted the little river, 'but I can't tell you where I'm going because I don't know myself. I'm hurrying to find out.' And on he went – gurgle, gurgle, splash, splash, plop, till he got to the foot of the hill.

There he saw people working in the fields, and children who came to paddle.

'Where have you come from and where are you going?' they asked. 'I've come from the top of the hill,' called the little river, 'but I can't tell you where I'm going because I don't know myself. I'm hurrying to find out. Good-bye.' And on he went – gurgle, gurgle, splash, splash, plop.

Soon he met other rivers, all hurrying along as fast as they could go. 'Let's join together,' they said, 'and make one big river.' So they did and made a great noise – swish, swish, swish – as they rushed along.

On and on they went, past villages and towns, over rocks and under bridges, until at last they came to the end of their travels. Where do you think that was? Why, the sea of course – the great wide beautiful sea!

So all the little rivers found out at last where they had been hurrying to all their long journey, and they shouted with joy as they plunged into the deep blue water.

'Here we are at last,' they said. 'This is where we belong,' and they joined in the song of the waves.

If you want to know what that sounds like, you must find a big shell and hold it to your ear, and listen very hard. Then you will hear for yourself the song of the sea.

From *More Stories to Tell to the Nursery*

The Traffic Jam

BY JILL MEILLON

Billy Brown's Daddy had a shiny blue car with silver shiny door handles. He had polished it to take Billy and his sister, Sue, to see a grand procession.

'Good-bye,' they called to Mummy, who was going to have a rest.

'Good-bye,' called Mummy.

Daddy started the engine, and out of the gate and down the street ran the shiny blue car.

'Hooray!' shouted Billy. 'I love processions!'

'So do I!' cried Sue. 'Specially if there is a band. Hurry, Daddy, hurry!'

But as Daddy turned into Main Street, there was traffic everywhere, and he couldn't hurry one bit. Soon he had to stop.

'Oh,' sighed Billy.

'Bother,' said Sue. 'Now we may be late for the procession.'

A baker's cart was standing right in front of them, so Mr Brown tooted his horn:

'Toot-toot . . . get out of my way.
We want to see the procession today.'

But the baker's van couldn't move because a big coal-lorry was standing right in front of it. The baker didn't want to stand there any longer, so he sounded his horn:

'Pyp-pyp, please do go,
You're holding the traffic up, you know.'

Now this made the driver of the coal-lorry very impatient. It wasn't his fault that he couldn't move. A taxi was standing right in front of him. So he honked his big horn at the taxi:

'Honk-honk . . . will you move ahead?
This coal in my truck is heavy as lead.'

But the taxi couldn't move an inch, for a high red bus had pulled up just in front of him. He tooted his horn:

'Peep–peep . . . you great red bus,
Start moving and stop all this fuss.'

But the high red bus stood still. The people on it popped their heads out of the windows. What a lot of noise they heard!

'What has happened?' asked everyone. But only the bus driver knew. He got out of his seat, and walked in front of the red bus. There on the roadway stood a frightened black kitten. Its soft black fur stood up all over it.

'Miaow,' it cried. 'I'm so frightened. Please take me across the road.'

The kindly bus driver picked up the kitten, and carried it across the road and put it safely on the footpath.

'Miaow,' said the kitten. 'Thank you!'

The people on the bus were glad their driver had been so kind and no one was cross any longer. Soon the bus driver was back in his seat. He started the engine and the bus began to move.

Then the taxi began to move . . . and the coal-lorry began to move . . . and the baker's van began to move . . . and Mr Brown's shiny blue car began to move.

'Hooray!' cried Billy and Sue.

'I'm glad the bus driver saved that little kitten,' said Sue.

'It doesn't really matter if we do miss a bit of the procession,' said Billy.

But they didn't miss any, really, and there were soldiers and a band and horses and all kinds of things. It was a *grand* procession.

From *Listening Time*

The Elves and the Shoemaker

TRADITIONAL

Once upon a time there was a shoemaker who became so poor that at last he had only enough money to buy leather for *one* pair of shoes. He cut them out carefully then went to bed, wondering how he was going to feed his family.

But when he got up in the morning, he found a beautiful pair of shoes on his work bench. Someone had made up the leather so well that when a customer came in, he bought the shoes at once and paid a good price for them.

Now the shoemaker had enough money to buy leather for *two* pairs of shoes, so he cut them out and laid them on his work bench ready for the morning.

Next day there were two pairs of shoes, with every stitch and nail put in perfectly.

'Whoever can it be that is helping us in this way?' said the shoemaker to his wife. But he bought enough leather for four pairs of shoes and cut them out as before.

In the morning, there were *four* pairs of fine shoes on the bench. And so it went on day after day until the shoemaker and his wife and children had good clothes to wear and plenty to eat. The shoes he sold were so fine that even the Queen bought a pair.

One day the shoemaker said to his wife: 'We *must* find out who is helping us, so that we can thank them. Let us stay awake tonight and see who it is.'

So they put leather on the bench as usual and then they hid and watched. At midnight, they heard voices and in through the door came two tiny men, not nearly as big as you. They were wearing pointed green caps but little else and their feet were bare. At once they began to work. Tap, tap, tap went their tiny hammers, in and out flew their needles and in no

time the shoes were done and the little men ran out into the cold night.

'Oh, husband,' said the wife, 'those poor little men have no shoes and hardly any clothes to keep them warm. Let us make them some clothes and shoes to show them how grateful we are.'

'Indeed yes, wife,' agreed the shoemaker.

So the wife made a fine white shirt for each and a green coat and trousers and knitted them a pair of green stockings each, while her husband cut and stitched and hammered at two pairs of tiny shoes, the best he could make.

Next night they hid again and watched, first spreading out their gifts for the little men. As the clock struck twelve, in came the tiny men and climbed on to the work bench to see what there was for them to do. When they saw the clothes and shoes, they chattered with excitement. They put on the shirts and green coats and trousers, they pulled on the stockings and shoes, then they began to dance. Tappety, tap they went all round the room, waving their green caps and bowing to each other in a comical way. Then, with a last skip and jump, they clattered out of the room and away down the garden path in the moonlight.

The little men never came back again to make shoes for the shoemaker and his wife, but it didn't really matter for the shoemaker was now able to make plenty of money. But he and his wife never forgot the kindness of the two little men in green and they often told their children the story.

Adapted from *Grimm's Fairy Tales*

The Little Tiger who Didn't Like Washing

BY STEPHANIE SALE (12½ YEARS OLD)

Once upon a time, to the East of the Great White Mountains, there lived a tiger. He had a wife who wasn't quite as big as he was and they had a baby tiger who was quite small. The baby tiger was very good. He was polite to his family and he

always ate and drank tidily. *But* he hated having his fur washed and brushed. All the same he loved being told 'Oh! What beautiful stripes!' and 'How handsome you are, little tiger!' and things like that.

One day the little tiger woke up very early while his Daddy and Mummy were still fast asleep. He thought, 'If I run away until suppertime, I might not have to be washed and brushed all day!' So he got up and crept out of the house and into the jungle which lay at the bottom of the garden. He felt very happy and jumped and skipped and rolled in the grass which was so green and tall.

After a time the little tiger began to feel rather lonely, so he sat down and waited for someone to come by and talk to him. And soon along came a butterfly. It was a yellow butterfly with blue and red on its wings, so the little tiger was very pleased because he liked that kind of butterfly.

'Hello!' said the baby tiger. 'I'm going to play with you.'

'All right,' said the butterfly and she flew from flower to flower with the little tiger close behind her. When he got tired they stopped playing and the little tiger said, 'That was fun!'

Then the butterfly said, 'Please will you tell me who you are? I can't remember seeing you before.'

'I'm a little tiger, of course. Can't you see my stripes?' said the little tiger.

'Stripes!' said the butterfly. 'I can't see any stripes at all,' and she flew away, leaving the little tiger alone again.

The little tiger went on along the path feeling very puzzled. Now he only did a few jumps and skips. By and by he met some monkeys who were sitting in a tree eating coconuts and chattering to each other.

'Can I play with you?' asked the little tiger.

'All right,' said the monkeys and they ran up and down the trees eating coconuts as they went. The little tiger tried to catch them when they touched the ground but he never could. When they were all tired out, the monkeys said, 'What kind of animal are you? We've never seen you before.'

'I'm a little tiger, of course. Can't you see my stripes?' said the little tiger anxiously.

'He says he's a tiger! He *hasn't* any stripes!' shouted the monkeys rudely and they threw a coconut at him which hurt him rather.

The little tiger went on slowly. He was thirsty so he padded along to the pool where his Mummy brought him each day when he had been washed and brushed. When he got there a green snake, that the little tiger knew quite well, was basking in the sun.

'Go away!' hissed the snake.

The little tiger stood still.

'Go away, yellow thing! I don't like strangers!' hissed the snake.

'I – I'm not a st-stranger,' said the little tiger, trying to be brave.

'You are, and if you don't go away you'll see what happens!' said the snake and he hissed rather loudly.

The little tiger put his tail between his legs and went to another part of the pool, which wasn't nearly so nice.

He looked into the pool and there he saw reflected a yellow fuzzy THING, all covered with bits of grass and dust. He knew now why the butterfly and the monkeys couldn't see any stripes on him and wouldn't believe he was a tiger. A great big tear rolled down his face, so he turned round and went home to tell his Mummy that he *did* want his fur brushed after all.

His Mummy was very glad to see him and she told him not to run away again. When she had washed his fur quite clean,

his stripes began to show up quite well. But when she had brushed him, his stripes were so black and shiny that he was very handsome indeed.

After that the little tiger loved having his fur washed and brushed and, when he was bigger, he learned to do it himself, for he wanted everyone to know that he was a tiger.

The Silver Horse

BY URSULA MORAY WILLIAMS

Christmas Eve and stars in the sky! Snow, snow everywhere, and the wide white world so quiet!

Inside the carpenter's shop six wooden hobby-horses stood beside the work bench, waiting for Santa Claus. One red, one blue, one green, one yellow, one purple and one white with spots, they all had round black eyes and scarlet wheels, of which they were very proud. Old Mr Tandy the carpenter had just finished making them.

Now he was tidying up his shop before going down the village street to eat a mince-pie and drink a cup of tea with old Mrs Higgins. The Christmas bells were ringing. In two hours it would be midnight and he wanted company.

Far away across the fields came the galloping hooves of a silver horse. It was the Christmas horse with a bag on its back, gathering up the naughtiness the children had thrown away before Santa Claus came.

All the children had said their prayers and begged pardon for their badness during the year. Now they were fast asleep in bed with their stockings hung up, smiling in their sleep.

The Christmas horse came galloping down the street to stick his head over the half-door of the carpenter's shop.

'Oh, you beautiful thing!' cried the hobby-horses, clattering to welcome him.

'I can't stay to play with you!' said the silver horse. 'I have hundreds of miles to go! Happy Christmas to you all! Goodbye!'

Away he went down the village street.

'What a pity!' said the hobby-horses, listening to the flying feet.

The smallest of the hobby-horses had nibbled a hole in the bag on the back of the silver horse. He wanted to find out what was inside it. And something had got out!

There in the snow where the silver horse had stood was a small round creature with bright eyes and turned-out toes. It was a bundle of badness belonging to Little Mikey.

Little Mikey was a boy who always ran away. He ran away from home, he ran away from school. When Christmas time came he made up his mind never to run away again. He had said he was sorry and thrown his naughtiness out of the window. Now it had escaped out of the bag on the back of the silver horse.

'Come out and play!' said Little Mikey, dancing in the snow.

'No! No! No!' said the hobby-horses.

'Just a little frisk in the fields! Just a little gallop in the snow!' said Little Mikey. 'Hark at the Christmas bells! There's lots of time before Santa comes! Come out with me!'

'No! No!' said all the hobby-horses. 'Old Mr Tandy would be very angry!'

'He wouldn't know!' said Little Mikey. 'Come out and try your scarlet wheels! Come out and stretch your wooden legs! Come out and jump in the snow and slide on the ice!'

'No!' said the hobby-horses.

'Then I shall go after the silver horse,' said Little Mikey, 'but now I shall never catch him up! I have wasted my time talking to you and I shall be left behind and never see him again, unless one of you lets me ride on your back, but of course not one of you is as fast as he!' and the little creature began to sniff.

The hobby-horses came trotting out of the workshop. They were sorry to see Little Mikey sad, and every one of them wished to prove that he could catch up with the silver horse. The leader took Little Mikey on his back and they galloped like the wind up the quiet village street.

Old Mr Tandy the carpenter was just finishing his cup of tea.

'What was that?' he said to Mrs Higgins. 'The Christmas horse has already gone by and it is still too early for Santa Claus. I had better be getting back to my workshop!'

But when Mr Tandy got back to his workshop the door

was wide open and the hobby-horses were gone! The poor old carpenter sat down with his head in his hands and cried.

Presently he wiped his eyes and blew his nose. 'Crying won't bring back my horses!' he said. 'I had better go and find them!'

He took a stick to walk with and a lantern off the peg to light his way. Then he tramped off up the village street to follow the hobby-horses and the silver horse.

Presently he had left the village behind, with all the lighted windows lit up by spangled Christmas trees. Frosty fields and woods stretched out before him, with snow-filled ditches and frozen streams.

The hobby-horses had left the road, and now their tracks led over hill and dale. They had jumped over hedges and leapt over ditches, and among the trails left by their scarlet wheels were the sharp clear hoof-prints of the silver horse.

Now and again Mr Tandy stooped down to pick up a fragment of broken braid, a wisp of mane torn by the branches, or even a battered wheel. Once he found a whole bridle hanging on a hedgerow, and the snow was stained with splinters of painted wood.

Old Mr Tandy tramped for miles, but he knew he would never catch up with the silver horse. Presently he turned round, and began slowly and painfully to make his way home again. His lantern went out, and his stick was broken, so he had to throw it away.

Half an hour before midnight he stumbled through the door and sat down to dry himself before a fire of wood-shavings. In a few minutes he was fast asleep.

Outside, the white world was quiet again under the snow, until far away across the fields came the galloping hooves of a silver horse. And with the galloping a tappeting and clattering as if wooden sticks were tapping and wooden wheels going round.

Nearer and nearer they came till they clattered down the village street. The workshop door was pushed open and the hobby-horses trotted in. Outside in the snow stood the silver horse whinnying a piercing whinny.

Old Mr Tandy woke with a start, and the first thing he saw was his six hobby-horses. But oh! what a state they were in! Their wheels were broken, their paint was scratched, their manes were torn and their legs were battered. And every one of them hung his head in shame and penitence. The silver horse had a hole in his bag and out of the bag were sticking the runaway legs of Little Mikey.

Old Mr Tandy did not stop to scold them. With his needle and thread he quickly stitched up the hole in case anything else should escape and cause mischief. Then he gave the silver horse a kindly clap on the back and away it galloped till the sound of its hooves could no longer be heard, while Mr Tandy set to work mending the reins and painting the legs and hammering new wheels on his hobby-horses, faster than he had worked in all his life before.

Two minutes before midnight the job was done, and only one thing was missing. The pretty red wheels they had all been so proud of had been replaced by plain white wooden ones. That was their punishment, and it would remind the hobby-horses never to run away again.

As the last wheel was fixed, the Christmas bells began to peal with a new and joyful sound, mingling with the tinkle of sleighbells and the patter of reindeer's feet.

Mr Tandy took his hobby-horses to the door. Then he kissed each one on the nose and stood waiting for Santa Claus and listening to the Christmas chimes across the sparkling snow, while the reindeer sleigh came nearer and nearer, and far, far away across the wide white world beyond the village galloped the silver horse.

Ride a Cock-horse

Ride a cock-horse to Banbury Cross,
To see a fine lady upon a white horse,
Rings on her fingers and bells on her toes,
She shall have music wherever she goes.

TRADITIONAL

Party Games

The children dance round in a ring, singing:

Here we go round the mulberry bush,
The mulberry bush, the mulberry bush.
Here we go round the mulberry bush
On a cold and frosty morning.

This is the way we wash our hands,
Wash our hands, wash our hands.
This is the way we wash our hands
On a cold and frosty morning.

Any kind of variant suggested by the children or the adults, will do – 'Brush our hair', 'Clap our hands', etc. The actions are suited to the words. The game ends with the singing of the first verse again.

LOOBY LOO
The children dance round singing:

Here we go looby loo,
Here we go looby light,
Here we go looby loo,
All on a Saturday night.

83

Standing still, they continue thus:

Put your left hand in,
Put your left hand out,
Shake it a little, a little,
And turn yourself about,

suiting the action to the words. Any variants can be used. In between each action, the chorus is sung again.

This may be quite a useful exercise as all children have to learn which *is* their right and left!

THE FARMER WANTS A WIFE

A 'farmer' is chosen and stands in the middle while the other children move round him singing. He chooses a 'wife' who joins him in the ring. She chooses a 'child', and so on. The climax, when everyone pats the 'dog', ends the game.

The words of the song are as follows:

The farmer wants a wife,
The farmer wants a wife,
Hey ho, hey ho,
The farmer wants a wife.

The wife wants a child,
The wife wants a child,
Hey ho, hey ho,
The wife wants a child.

84

The child wants a nurse,
The child wants a nurse,
Hey ho, hey ho,
The child wants a nurse.

The nurse wants a dog,
The nurse wants a dog,
Hey ho, hey ho,
The nurse wants a dog.

The dog wants a bone,
The dog wants a bone,
Hey ho, hey ho,
The dog wants a bone.

We all pat the dog,
We all pat the dog,
Hey ho, hey ho,
We all pat the dog.

FOX AND GEESE

This is a game that needs plenty of room, so it should be played in the garden if possible.

Mother Goose is an older child and the smaller children line up behind her. She spreads her arms to protect them and

faces Mr Fox. He tries to get beyond Mother Goose and to reach the child at the end of the wildly swaying line of children who clasp each other round the waist. The captured 'goslings' are out of the game which goes on until the children or Mr Fox tire.

The Bus That Wouldn't Go

BY MARGARET LAW

One morning Red Bus woke up in a very bad temper. 'I'm tired of always having to get up so early,' he grumbled. 'I'm tired of having to go out on wet cold mornings. I'm tired of carrying people to their work. In fact I've made up my mind that I'm not going to do it any more.' So when his driver came to fetch him he just wouldn't start. He stood quite still in front of the garage door, so that none of the other buses could get out either.

'Now, now,' said his driver, 'come along, old fellow. Get a move on do, or we'll be late at the first stop.'

'As if *I* cared about that!' snorted the bus and made rude noises in his inside. His driver got down from his seat and lifted the bonnet to see if he could find out what was wrong, but every time he touched anything the bus went sputter-sputter-spit back at him in a very angry manner. The poor man scratched his head and then he turned a big handle at the front. Bang! bang! bang! splutter! went the bus but he didn't move an inch.

The other buses began to get angry because they could not get out of the garage. They started blowing their horns and shouting at Red Bus to get out of the way, but he pretended

not to hear them. He stood firmly in the middle of the door-way and would not budge.

Outside at the first bus stop all the people were waiting.

'What has happened?' they asked each other. 'Red Bus is never late. He always comes on time,' and they looked anxiously along the road.

'I'll miss my train,' said the tall man.

'I won't be able to open my shop,' said the short one.

'I won't get to my office,' said the pretty girl.

'We won't be able to go to school!' said the children. 'Hurrah!'

Then they all said, 'Hurry up, Red Bus – *do*.'

But the bus didn't come. He was still standing in front of the garage door. The driver stood amongst all the other bus drivers talking things over, and at last one of them had a good idea.

'There's a door at the back,' he said. 'It's smaller than the front one, but Red Bus is much bigger than any of the other buses, so I think that if we took down the posts at each side they might manage to get through. We'll show old Grumpy we can do without him.'

When Red Bus heard that, he came out of his sulks in a hurry, and he started to make his engine run, as if he would be off at any moment.

'Bless my soul!' said his driver. 'Do you hear that?' and he climbed up into the driver's seat and grasped the wheel just as Red Bus rolled out on to the road.

'Do without me indeed! I'll let them see if they do,' he spluttered and fairly raced along the street.

When the people at the bus stop saw him coming they waved and shouted. 'Good old Reddy,' they cried. 'We knew you'd turn up,' and they piled inside.

'I'll catch my train,' said the tall man.

'I'll open my shop,' said the short fat one.

'I'll get to my office,' said the pretty girl.

'We'll be in time for school,' said the children.

Between you and me, Red Bus felt very ashamed of himself when he saw how pleased the people were to see him and how fond of him they all were.

'I can't think what was the matter with me,' he said. 'Perhaps my driver was right and I needed more oil in my inside.'

I can tell you that Red Bus was never, never late again.

From *Stories to Tell to the Nursery*

The Hot Potato

BY DONALD BISSET

Once upon a time there lived a cow whose name was Dot, who was very fond of hot potatoes. One day she swallowed one whole without chewing it, and it was so hot inside her that it hurt, and she began to cry. Great big tears rolled down her cheeks.

The farmer, whose name was Mr Smith, got a bucket to catch her tears in, so that they wouldn't make the floor all wet.

'Whatever is the matter, Dot?' he said. 'I swallowed a hot potato,' said Dot. 'You poor thing,' said Mr Smith, 'open your mouth.' Dot opened her mouth and smoke came out. What was to be done!

Mr Smith picked up the bucket of tears and poured it down Dot's throat. There was a sort of sizzling noise, and Dot smiled because she felt better.

That evening, when Dot was lying in her byre, eating some hay, she made up a song:

> When you eat potatoes hot,
> Be sure you chew them quite a lot
> Or you'll get a pain inside,
> Like the time I did and cried,
> Because I didn't stop to chew
> My potato through and through.
> What a silly cow I am!
> What a silly cow I am!

And that is all Dot wrote because, just then, she fell asleep.

From *Some Time Stories*

The Sky is Falling

TRADITIONAL

One day Henny Penny was walking in the woods when an acorn fell on her little head. 'Oh,' she said, 'the sky is falling! I must go and tell the King.'

So she set out and on the way she met Cocky Locky. 'Where are you going?' asked Cocky Locky.

'Oh, the sky is falling!' said Henny Penny. 'I am going to tell the King.'

'Then I'll come with you,' said Cocky Locky.

On they went together and they met Ducky Daddles. 'Where are you going?' she asked.

'Oh, I met Henny Penny,' said Cocky Locky, 'and she says the sky is falling! So we are going to tell the King.'

'I'll come with you,' said Ducky Daddles.

They walked on together and they met Goosey Poosey. 'Where are you going?' he asked.

'I met Cocky Locky,' said Ducky Daddles, 'and he met Henny Penny and she says the sky is falling! So we are going to tell the King.'

'Then I'll come with you,' said Goosey Poosey.

They hurried on and they met Turkey Lurkey. 'Where are you going?' he asked.

'Oh,' said Goosey Poosey, 'I met Ducky Daddles and she met Cocky Locky and he met Henny Penny and she says the sky is falling! So we are going to tell the King.'

'I'll come with you,' said Turkey Lurkey.

They all travelled on until they met Foxy Woxy. 'Where are you going?' he asked.

'Oh,' said Turkey Lurkey, 'I met Goosey Poosey and he met Ducky Daddles and she met Cocky Locky and he met Henny Penny and she says the sky is falling! So we are going to see the King.'

'I'll come with you and show you the quickest way,' said Foxy Woxy.

They came to a dark hole. 'This way,' said Foxy Woxy and he led them into his den.

And that was the end of Turkey Lurkey, Goosey Poosey, Ducky Daddles and Cocky Locky. But Henny Penny didn't go into Foxy Woxy's den, she ran home and stayed there.

So the King never knew the sky was falling.

To the Stars

BY VERA COLWELL

Nearly every day if it was fine, Paul went to the Park with his mother and his baby sister. One Spring day when the sun was shining and the wind chasing the white clouds across the sky, they set out as usual. When they got to the Park gates they had a surprise. The Balloon Man was there.

He was holding the strings of dozens of balloons and they were all tugging as if they were trying to fly away. Some were blue, others yellow or red; some were ordinary shapes and others were like strange animals.

'Oh, Mummy,' said Paul, 'can I buy a balloon, please? I've got threepence that Uncle gave me.'

'Of course, darling,' said Mummy. 'A windy day like this is just right for balloons. I'll choose one for Baby Sister and you choose your own.'

So Mummy bought a balloon that looked like a duck and tied it on to the handle of the pram where it danced about in the wind. Baby Sister waved her hands about and gurgled with delight.

Paul found it very difficult to make up his mind. There were so many fine balloons. Then he saw the best one of all – it was blue with beautiful silver stars. He paid his threepence and ran along with the balloon bobbing behind him just as if it was enjoying itself as much as Paul. The wind was blowing so hard, Paul just had to run and run until he got to the lake.

So much was happening there that Paul tied his balloon to the railing so that he could watch better. There were some ducks with bright blue and green feathers and one of them was standing on its head in the water. In a quiet corner of the

lake, a mother duck was swimming along with six little ducklings paddling along behind her. Toy boats were scudding across the water with the wind behind them.

Suddenly Paul noticed a blue balloon bouncing about on the water. It had silver stars on it just like his – Gracious! It *was* his! The knot he had tied had come undone and the blue balloon had escaped.

The ducks quacked in fright, the one that was standing on its head turned right way up in a hurry as the balloon bumped into its tail. A toy boat caught in the string of the balloon and away it went across the lake with the blue balloon flying behind it like a flag. Smack! The boat crashed into the bank. Luckily a big boy managed to disentangle the string and Paul got his balloon back again.

'I think this balloon is fun,' said Paul. 'I wonder what it will do next!'

Paul held on tightly to the blue balloon as it tugged to get away again. He walked by the side of the pram until Peter, a friend of his, came along.

'That's a good balloon,' said Peter. 'Let's play with it.'

'It's a very bouncy balloon,' said Paul.

So it was. They ran after it and wouldn't let it bounce too high, but several times it nearly blew away. Then suddenly the wind caught it and lifted it into the air. Paul jumped and missed it. Peter tried to catch the string and missed it.

'Catch it!' they shouted and a tall man who was passing

by reached up his long arm, but he missed the balloon too.

It rose still higher. A workman who was climbing a ladder set against a tree leaned out and made a grab at the blue balloon as it floated by. He, too, missed it.

Now everyone was looking up at the little blue balloon. Every time it dropped a little, children ran to catch it, but it always floated out of reach.

Now the blue balloon was higher than the tree and higher than the houses. It rose up and up with the sun shining on it until it could hardly be seen at all. Then it flew quite out of sight.

'It's gone!' said Paul sadly. 'Where do you think it is going, Mummy?'

'Perhaps to the seaside,' said Mummy.

'It had stars on it,' said Paul. '*I* think it's flying right up to the stars . . .'

Who knows?

Wee Willie Winkie

Wee Willie Winkie runs through the town,
Upstairs and downstairs in his nightgown.
Rapping at the window, crying through the lock,
'Are the children in their beds?
It's past eight o'clock.'

Chunky the China Pig

BY GLENYS EVANS

In a shop window there lived three china pigs. Two of them belonged to each other and sat on a little tray. They were called Pepper and Salt. The other one was called Chunky. He was a money-box really and he had a slit along his back for the money to go through. But he had been empty for so long that his nice curly tail had grown quite straight and his happy smile had gone.

Pepper and Salt were very unkind to Chunky.

'Nobody will ever buy you,' said Pepper, 'because you look so unhappy.'

'And what use are you anyway!' said Salt. 'Pepper and I are *very* useful. We sit on the table when people have their meals and we make their food taste nicer.'

This made Chunky feel so sad that a large china tear began to roll down his cheek. Just at that moment an old lady came into the shop.

'I would like to buy that unhappy pig, please,' said the old lady. 'I think my grandson, Willie, would think it was fun to drop his pennies into that little pig.' So the shopkeeper wrapped up Chunky very carefully in soft paper and the old lady took him away.

But when she got home and showed Chunky to her grandson, Willie said: 'I don't like him, Granny. He looks so unhappy and his tail is straight instead of curly.'

'Never mind,' said Granny. 'Put this penny inside him.'

So Willie pushed the penny through the slit in Chunky's back and it went *clink* inside his china tummy. 'Oh!' said Willie. 'I like that noise.'

After that Granny gave Willie a penny every Saturday to put inside the china pig and slowly Chunky began to get quite heavy. Each day he felt happier and happier and one day he even tried to smile! Something else happened too – Chunky's tail began to curl! First the end turned up, then, as more money was pushed through Chunky's back, the curl became tighter.

Willie was very excited. He looked at Chunky every day and saved every penny he got to put inside the little pig. *Clink . . . clink . . . clink* they fell down inside Chunky's tummy until he was quite full. Now he was very happy and smiled all day and his tail was in a tight curl.

So Willie loved his little china pig very much and he was always careful to keep him full of pennies. He knew that if he forgot, Chunky's tail might grow straight again and he might stop smiling. That would *never* do!

The Big Red Apple

BY MARJORIE POPPLETON

Once upon a time there was a little boy, and one day he put on his blue coat and his red cap and he went for a walk, up hill and down dale.

Now in his blue coat there was a pocket, and in his pocket there was a big red apple which his mother had given him.

Soon the little boy came to a steep hill and he began to run down it, jiggety-jog. And as he ran the big red apple in the pocket of his blue coat began to slip, and it slipped and slipped until it fell out of the pocket on to the ground and went rolling, rolling, down the hill – bumpety-bump!

Now the little boy could run fast, but he couldn't run as fast as the apple could roll. So the apple rolled on and on until it was out of sight and the little boy wondered wherever he would find his big red apple again.

The apple rolled on and on until by and by it came to the bottom of the hill, and there it fell – PLOP, splash – into a pond.

But the apple didn't sink when it fell into the pond. It bobbed up and down on top of the water. And presently two fish swam up to look at it. They sucked at it and they blew little bubbles at it, to find out if it was good to eat. And then it seemed as though they said:

'Pooh, pooh!
We wouldn't eat you!'

And off they swam to look for something they did like.

And all this time the little boy was coming down the hill wondering *wherever he would find his big red apple again*.

Next a frog came swimming along. 'Here's a fine red apple,' said he. 'I don't like apples to eat but I can use this one

to sit on.' So the frog tried to climb on to the apple, but every time he tried, the apple rolled over and he slipped into the water again – SPLASH!

By this time the apple had floated across the pond and it was coming close to the other side. But the little boy hadn't yet come to the pond and he didn't know his apple was there. But *somebody* had come to the pond and was looking at the apple, and that was Mr Grey Squirrel.

Mr Grey Squirrel watched the apple come floating nearer and he said: 'It is evidently time for me to eat, and today I think I will have a BIG RED APPLE.'

So Mr Grey Squirrel put one paw on the apple, and then he put two paws on the apple and pulled it out of the pond and on to the grass. And he stuck his teeth in it.

And all this time the little boy in the blue coat and the red cap was coming down the hill wondering *wherever he would find his big red apple again.*

'I must take this apple to the top of a tree,' said Mr Grey Squirrel, 'or somebody will get it.' So he began to climb up a tree with the little boy's apple in his mouth.

Now just then the little boy reached the bottom of the hill and ran to the edge of the pond. He looked in the pond for his apple, but it wasn't there. And then he looked everywhere, until at last he saw Mr Grey Squirrel up in the tree, and he saw the big red apple in Mr Grey Squirrel's mouth.

'Give me my apple,' shouted the little boy. But Mr Squirrel didn't answer. His mouth was too full.

Then the little boy clapped his hands and made such a clatter that Mr Grey Squirrel was frightened and let the apple fall to the ground.

So the little boy ran and picked up his apple. And he said: 'I wonder what Mr Grey Squirrel will have for dinner now.'

And he looked up, and there was Mr Grey Squirrel sitting on a branch right above him and looking very hungry indeed.

Then the little boy took one big bite out of his apple and he put the rest of it on the ground at the foot of the tree.

'Squirrel, Squirrel,' he cried. 'Your dinner is ready, and I see that there is a BIG RED APPLE for you today.'

Well, the Squirrel didn't need telling twice. Down the tree he came, in a great hurry. And then the little boy ran home in a great hurry too – to eat his own dinner and tell his mother all that had happened to the BIG RED APPLE she gave him.

From *Ten Tales for the Very Young*

I Had a Little Nut Tree

I had a little nut tree,
Nothing would it bear
But a silver nutmeg
And a golden pear;
The King of Spain's daughter
Came to visit me,
And all for the sake
Of my little nut tree.

Punchinello Kept a Cat

BY JEAN CHAPMAN

Punchinello was not only the funniest clown in all the circus, he was the happiest.

He lived in a little yellow caravan that had wheels as bright as spinning-tops. In the caravan lived Punchinello's little friend, a little grey cat called Tillica.

All the circus people liked Punchinello. All the circus people liked Tillica; that is, everyone except the Ring-master.

The Ringmaster had a big, bellowing voice. As he walked past the yellow caravan, he roared as loud as the lions. 'Punchinello! Punchinello!'

Hearing that voice Punchinello put his hands over his ears to keep out some of the roar. And hearing that voice Tillica hid under the bedspread.

'Punchinello!' shouted the Ringmaster. 'I hear you have a cat. We can't have a cat in this circus.'

'But why?' asked Punchinello, poking his head out through the window. 'Tillica is a very nice cat.'

'We can't keep a cat in the circus, because people don't want to see a cat,' the Ringmaster told him. 'A cat can't do tricks like a bear or a monkey.'

Of course Punchinello didn't want to send his little Tillica away. He tried to teach her to do tricks like the circus dogs. But all Tillica did was rub her smooth head against his baggy trousers.

The fat man who trained the seal to balance a ball on the tip of his nose came and tried to teach Tillica to balance a ball on the tip of *her* nose. But all Tillica did was to chase the ball and push it with her little white paw.

The thin man who taught the lions to sit still on their boxes came and tried to teach Tillica to stand on her hind legs and

dance. But all Tillica would do was walk on her four paws with her tail in the air.

The little dark man who taught the elephants to walk in a circle, holding each other's tails with their trunks, tried to teach Tillica to jump through a paper hoop. But Tillica just licked her paw with a pink tongue and washed her face.

'Too bad,' they all sighed to Punchinello, 'Tillica can't do tricks. She's just an ordinary little grey cat.'

But Punchinello had thought of an idea.

At the next performance of the circus, he didn't run into the ring with the red pompons on his cap a-bobbing and his long flat feet a-flapping. Instead he staggered in under the biggest basket ever made.

'Whatever is in that basket?' shouted the Ringmaster.

'Lift up the lid and see,' Punchinello told him.

The Ringmaster opened the lid and pulled out another basket that was just a little bit smaller. 'What's in this basket?' he asked.

'Look and see!' said Punchinello.

The Ringmaster found another basket inside, then another and another. Soon there were baskets all over the circus-ring. By now the children were standing in their seats and craning their necks to see what could be in the basket.

Then there came a basket that wasn't very big and it wasn't very high. The Ringmaster lifted the lid – inside sat Tillica, cleaning her whiskers!

'Ooooooooooh!' said the children with mouths as round as oranges. 'Do it again! Do it again!'

So, instead of frowning, the Ringmaster beamed a smile from ear to ear.

As a matter of fact, soon he was thinking it had been his idea to let Tillica surprise the children in this wonderful game.

And so Punchinello kept his cat.

From *Listening Time*

Pussy Sits by the Fire

Pussy sits by the fire,
So pretty and so fair.
In walks the little dog,
Ah, Pussy, are you there?

How do you do, Mistress Pussy?
Mistress Pussy, how do you do?
I thank you kindly, little dog,
I'm very well just now.

The Tale of the Little Brown Bird

BY ELIZABETH CLARK

Once upon a time there was a little Brown Bird, and he was very unhappy because he had broken his wing. He did not like to have to go hop, hop, hop, until his wing got well, instead of flying through the air. But what was worse still was that winter was coming. Soon the North Wind would go roaring through the woods, shaking the leaves from the trees, bringing the snow, and covering the blue sky with grey clouds. Each day some of the little Brown Bird's friends spread their wings and flew away to warm countries where there was plenty of food for little birds to eat all through the winter. At last the little Brown Bird was left all alone, and he was very unhappy indeed.

'What shall I do?' said the little Brown Bird, 'with no friends to talk to all through the long, cold winter.' And then he had a bright idea. 'I will ask a tree to take care of me,' he said, 'till the Spring comes back again.'

So off he went, hop, hop, hop, with his broken wing, till he came to the Silver Birch tree. Now the Silver Birch is a very pretty tree with a silvery white trunk and long slender branches that wave in the wind, and little green leaves that twinkle when the sun shines on them.

And the little Brown Bird said to himself, 'What a pretty lady! She is sure to be kind to me.' And he called, 'Lady Birch! I'm a little Brown Bird with a broken wing. May I sit among your branches till the Spring comes again?'

But the Silver Birch wasn't kind to him at all. She said, 'Certainly *not*. Go away, little Bird.'

Well, the little Brown Bird was very disappointed, but he said to himself, 'I *must* find a tree to sit in.' So he went hop, hop, hop, till he came to the big Oak Tree. Now the Oak is very big and strong with branches that spread out far and wide; and when the little Brown Bird looked at him he said to himself, 'He looks so big and strong, he must be kind.' And he called: "Father Oak! I'm a little Brown Bird with a broken wing. May I sit among your branches till the Spring comes back again?'

But the Oak said in his big voice, 'Certainly *not*. If I let you sit among my branches you might eat my acorns!'

Well, the little Brown Bird was very disappointed, but he said to himself, 'I *must* find a tree to sit in.' So he went hop, hop, hop, till he came to the Weeping Willow. Now the Weeping Willow was bending and trailing her branches in the river. And the little Brown Bird said to himself, 'She looks rather sad, perhaps she'll be kind to me.' And he called, 'Lady Willow! I'm a little Brown Bird with a broken wing. May I sit among your branches till the Spring comes back again?'

But the Weeping Willow only waved her branches and

said, 'Go-oo-oo-oo awa-a-y, Little Bird. I've got troubles of my own!'

The poor little Brown Bird was so unhappy that he didn't know what to do. He sat there with all his brown feathers fluffed out, looking very miserable indeed. And then he heard a kind voice, a warm voice, and it said, 'Little Bird! My branches are thick and cosy. Hop up and keep warm among them till the Spring comes again.'

It was the Fir tree. The little Brown Bird hopped up into its branches and was just about to put his head under his wing when he heard another voice.

This time it was a rather creaky voice, but a kind one, and it said: 'Lit-tle Bird! I – can – keep – the – wind – off.' It was the tall Pine tree. It was swaying to and fro in the wind and it did keep the wind off the little Brown Bird.

He was just going off to sleep when he heard another voice, quite a little voice saying, 'Little Bird! My berries are good to eat.' It was the Juniper tree that grows close to the ground. The little Brown Bird remembered that he was hungry and he hopped down and had a good breakfast of Juniper berries. Then he hopped back into the Fir tree's branches and the Pine kept the wind off him and he put his head under his wing and went fast asleep.

That night the North Wind went roaring through the woods. He blew Lady Silver Birch about till her pretty green leaves came down and lay in a golden shower round her silver trunk. He tossed Father Oak until all his leaves and his acorns too were lying on the ground. And he sent all the Weeping Willow's leaves floating down the river. But he never touched the Fir or the Pine or the Juniper tree. They stayed fresh and green all the winter, and took care of the little Brown Bird.

And when Spring came back again, the little Brown Bird's broken wing was well and strong so that he could fly about with the other birds.

From *More Stories and How to Tell Them*

The North Wind Doth Blow

The North wind doth blow,
And we shall have snow,
And what will poor robin do then, poor thing?
He'll sit in a barn,
To keep himself warm,
And hide his head under his wing, poor thing.

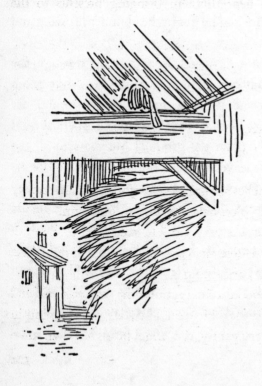

How the Fir Tree became our Christmas Tree

TRADITIONAL

When the Christ Child was born, all people and animals, and even the trees, felt a great happiness.

Outside the stable where the Baby was lying, there stood three trees, a Palm tree, an Olive tree and a little Fir tree. Each day people passed beneath them bringing presents to the Baby.

'We should like to give him presents too,' said the trees.

'I shall give him my biggest leaf,' said the tall Palm tree. 'When the hot weather comes, it will fan him and bring cool breezes.'

Said the Olive tree: 'I will give him sweet-smelling oil.'

'But what can I give him?' asked the little Fir tree anxiously.

'You! Your branches are prickly and your tears are sticky,' said the other trees. 'You have nothing to give him.'

The little Fir tree was very sad. He tried hard to think of something he could give that the Christ Child might like, but he had nothing good enough.

Now an Angel had heard everything the trees had said and he was sorry for the little Fir tree. The stars were shining in the night sky, so, very gently, the Angel brought down some of the smallest and brightest of them and put them on the prickly branches of the Fir tree.

Inside the stable, the Baby was lying awake. He could see the three trees against the night sky. Suddenly the dark green branches of the little Fir tree shone and sparkled, for the stars

were resting there like candles. How beautiful the little Fir tree seemed now!

And the Christ Child waved his hands, as babies do, and smiled.

And ever since the Fir tree has been the children's Christmas tree.

Good Night

Good night! Good night!
Far flies the light;
But still God's love
Shall flame above,
Making all bright.
Good night! Good night!

VICTOR HUGO

MAGIC
IN THE AIR

Phyllis Arkle

**People miss a lot, not believing
in magic.**

Sam believes in magic, and he's the only
person in the town who sees Weathervane
Witch fly off on her magic broomstick. It
doesn't take Sam long to find out why:
thieves have come to steal wild birds'
eggs, and the four precious eggs in
Golden Eagle's nest are in danger. But
with Sam and Weathervane Dragon's
help, Weathervane Witch is determined to
foil the robbers!

Also in Young Puffin

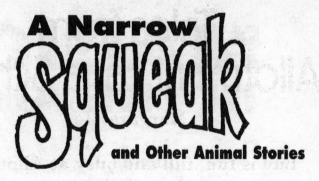

A Narrow Squeak

and Other Animal Stories

Dick King-Smith

**Be they soft and furry, sharp and prickly
or smooth and scaly, all the animals in
this collection are quite irresistible!**

A mouse is dicing with death in the larder,
while another is carried off in the jaws of a
fox. Then there's a bullied brontosaurus,
a wimpish woodlouse, a rebellious hedgehog
and a dog with an identity crisis.

'Other writers who put words into animals'
mouths are outclassed' – *The Times
Educational Supplement*

Also in Young Puffin

Tales from Allotment Lane School

Margaret Joy

Life is fun, full and busy at Allotment Lane School.

Twelve delightful stories, bright, light and funny, about the children in Miss Mee's class at Allotment Lane School. Meet Ian, the avid collector; meet Mary and Gary, who have busy mornings taking messages; and meet the school caterpillars, who disappear and turn up again in surprising circumstances.